SEAHORSES

Heinemann Library
Chicago, Illinois

Elizabeth Laskey

Designed by Kimberly Saar, Heinemann Library
Illustrations and maps by John Fleck
Photo research by Bill Broyles
Originated by Ambassador Litho Ltd.
Printed by Wing King Tong in Hong Kong

07 06 05 04 03
10 9 8 7 6 5 4 3 2 1

Library of Congress Cataloging-in-Publication Data
Laskey, Elizabeth, 1961-
    Seahorses / Elizabeth Laskey.
        p. cm. -- (Sea creatures)
Summary: Describes the physical characteristics, behavior, and habitat
of sea horses, as well as ways in which scientists study them.
Includes bibliographical references (p.   ).
    ISBN 1-40340-963-3 (IHC), 1-4034-3565-0 (pbk.)
    1. Sea horses--Juvenile literature. [1. Sea horses.] I. Title. II.
Series.
    QL638.S9 L37 2003
    597'.6798--dc21

                    2002010624

Acknowledgments
The author and publishers are grateful to the following for permission to reproduce copyright material:

Cover photograph by Doug Perrine/Seapics.com

Title page, pp. 4, 7, 14, 15, 16, 17, icons Rudie Kuiter/Seapics.com; pp. 5L, 10 Edward Lines/John G. Shedd Aquarium/Visuals Unlimited; p. 5R Tom & Pat Leeson/Photo Researchers, Inc.; p. 8 James D. Watt/Seapics.com; p. 9 Ken Lucas/Ardea; p. 11 Bob Cranston/Norbert Wu Photography; p. 12 David Wrobel/Visuals Unlimited; pp. 13, 28 David Kearnes/Seapics.com; pp. 18, 19T Fred Bavendam/Minden Pictures; p. 19B Doug Perrine/Seapics.com; p. 20 Guy Stubbs, Inc.; p. 21 K. B. Sandved/Visuals Unlimited; pp. 22, 23, 24 The Rolex Awards for Enterprise/Tomas Bertelsen; p. 25 John Makely/The Baltimore Sun; p. 26 George Grall/National Geographic Society; pp. 27, 29 Ken Lucas/Visuals Unlimited
Special thanks to Sarah Foster for her help in the preparation of this book.

Every effort has been made to contact copyright holders of any material reproduced in this book. Any omissions will be rectified in subsequent printings if notice is given to the publisher.

Some people spell seahorse as two words. Most scientists, however, spell it as one word. It is spelled as one word in this book.

Some words are shown in bold, **like this.** You can find out what they mean by looking in the glossary.

Contents

Where Would You Find a Seahorse?

You're standing on a beach in New South Wales, Australia, wearing a diving suit and a snorkel. In the water just offshore are White's seahorses. Today, you are going to try to find one. You slip into the sea and start swimming.

After about an hour, you finally spot a seahorse almost hidden among some sea plants. Now you know why it's called a seahorse. The creature's head looks just like a horse's head! But the seahorse's whole body is only about the length of a crayon. You take a closer look. It has a pouch like a kangaroo. And its tail is curled tightly around a sea plant the same way a monkey uses its tail to hang from a tree. What a strange creature!

Most White's seahorses live among sea plants. But some have been found living on underwater nets used to keep sharks away from beaches where people swim.

What Kind of Creature Is a Seahorse?

A seahorse is a fish. All fish, including seahorses, have certain features that are the same.

An unusual fish

All fish have **backbones.** A seahorse's backbone stretches from the bottom of its skull to the tip of its tail. All fish also breathe through **gills.** They all use **fins** to swim. If you look closely you will see that seahorses have all these fish features.

There is one other fish feature that you can't see. Seahorses, like all other fish, are **cold-blooded.** This means that they cannot control the temperature of their blood. Their blood matches the temperature of the water that they swim in. If the water gets warmer or colder, then a seahorse's blood will also warm up or cool down.

These seahorses and this trout don't look much alike, but they are both fish. Each has a backbone, gills, and fins.

How Many Kinds of Seahorses Are There?

Scientists know of at least 32 **species,** or types, of seahorses. Seahorses are found in all of the world's oceans except near the North and South Poles. It is too cold for them there. Seahorses do not like very deep water. They live near the coasts where it is shallow.

Four species live in North and South America

Only four species of seahorse are found off the shores of North and South America. The lined seahorse lives in the Atlantic Ocean. It can be found as far north as Canada. The longsnouted seahorse is also found in the Atlantic but only as far north as North Carolina and then as far south as Brazil. Another Atlantic species, the dwarf seahorse, makes its home near Florida and farther south. The large Pacific seahorse lives in the Pacific Ocean off the coast of California to as far south as Peru in South America.

There are more species of seahorses along Australia's coast than anywhere else in the world.

At least ten species live in Australia

At least ten species of seahorse live along Australia's coast. One is the potbelly seahorse. It has a belly like a little balloon. Other interesting seahorses close to Australia are the pygmy seahorse and the zebra seahorse.

The pygmy seahorse is one of the smallest seahorses. It is about three-fourths of an inch (two centimeters) long, or about as long as a piece of uncooked macaroni. The zebra seahorse has black and white stripes like a zebra.

Potbelly seahorses like these can be white, yellow, or brown.

Some species live in other parts of the world

If you travel north of Australia, watch out for the thorny seahorse. It is covered with prickly spines! Farther north, you might spot the tiger tail seahorse near the Philippines. It has a yellow and black striped tail.

If you are in southern Africa, you might see the rare Cape seahorse. It has a dark spot on its head and more spots on its back. Near Spain, France, or England, you might find the shortsnouted seahorse.

Which Habitats Do Seahorses Live In?

Different **species** of seahorse live in different types of surroundings, or **habitats.**

Seagrass beds, coral reefs, and mangrove forests

Species such as White's seahorse and the lined seahorse live in **seagrass beds.** Seagrass is a grassy plant that grows underwater. It often forms a thick "forest" of grass. Seahorses wrap their tails around seagrass and may not budge for hours!

The zebra seahorse and the pygmy seahorse live in **coral reefs.** Coral reefs are made of the skeletons of millions of tiny sea animals. Coral can have lots of tiny branches. These branches make good **holdfasts** where seahorses can hang out for a while.

The yellow seahorse lives in **mangrove forests** made up of groups of mangrove trees. Mangrove trees grow in shallow water along the seacoast. Mangroves' roots curve up and connect to the trees above the water.

The pygmy seahorse is very picky about where it lives. Only a certain type of coral, known as a sea fan, will do.

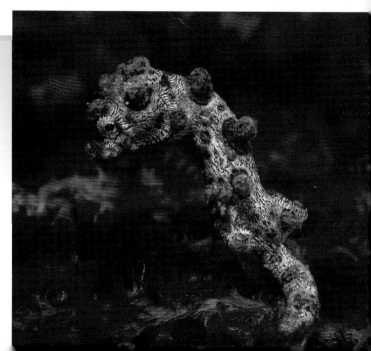

How Does a Seahorse's Body Work?

When you look at a seahorse, you will see a few things that look familiar, like the eyes and the tail. Other body parts don't look familiar at all. The seahorse's different body parts help it see, breathe, eat, and swim.

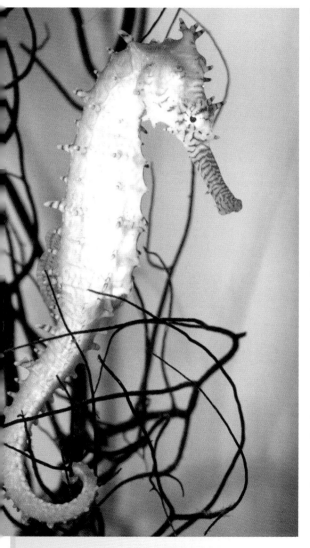

The thorney seahorse's coronet can be clearly seen on top of its head.

The coronet is on top of the head

The little crown on top of a seahorse's head is called a **coronet.** Most seahorses have coronets. Each seahorse's coronet is different from that of any other seahorse. The coronet also differs from species to species.

The eyes stay on the move

Seahorses have two eyes just like you do. Unlike you, a seahorse can move each eye in a different direction. It might keep one eye pointed forward to look for food. The other eye might be aimed backward, on the lookout for danger.

The snout sucks up food

The **snout** is a hollow tube like a straw. The seahorse uses it to suck up food. Snouts can be long or short. The shortsnouted seahorse, as you might guess, has a shorter snout than most other seahorse **species.**

Fins are for swimming

Seahorses have two **pectoral fins** that look like little wings on each side of the neck. On a seahorse's back is the **dorsal fin.** These three fins help the seahorse swim. Seahorses swim with the head pointed up and the tail pointed down. They move forward by flapping the dorsal fin very fast. The pectoral fins also move very fast. They help the seahorse steer and balance.

But seahorses are not fast swimmers. If a seahorse swam from one end of a bathtub to the other, it would take about five minutes.

To swim forward, this Pacific seahorse can flap its dorsal fin 35 times per second.

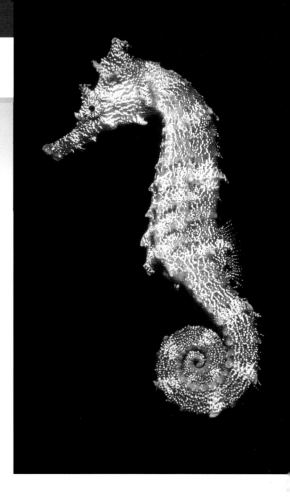

Seahorse tails curl in toward the front of the body, never away from the body. This is a thorny seahorse.

? **Did you know?**

If a seahorse wants to move up or down like an elevator, it simply rolls or unrolls its tail.

Gills are for breathing

Just above the pectoral fins are tiny **gill** openings. The gills help seahorses get oxygen from the water so they can breathe.

The tail is for hanging on

Seahorses use their tails mostly for hanging on to a piece of seagrass, a bit of coral, or even another seahorse! Because they are not very good at swimming, seahorses avoid doing it. This is where their tails come in handy. Most fish swim around looking for food. Seahorses let the food come to them. They simply find a **holdfast** to wrap their tail around and wait for food to float by. When not wrapped around a holdfast, the seahorse may keep its tail tightly curled.

What Do Seahorses Eat?

For seahorses, dinner lasts all day. Most seahorses wrap their tails around a **holdfast** and spend the day gobbling up sea animals, called **zooplankton,** that float by.

Shrimp, shrimp, and more shrimp

One favorite type of zooplankton are shrimp-like **crustaceans.** Huge numbers of these tiny animals live in **seagrass beds.** This works out very well for the **species** of seahorses that also happen to live there. Seahorses have been known to eat more than 3,000 of these shrimp between dawn and dusk.

This tiny crustacean is barely 1 inch (2.5 centimeters) long. Some of the larger seahorses can eat this shrimp. If the food will fit in the opening of its snout, the seahorse will eat it.

Seahorses have strong upper and lower jaws that can open and close the snout with lightning-fast speed.

When a seahorse spots a food item, it begins sucking the tiny animal toward its snout. As soon as the zooplankton enters the snout, the seahorse snaps the snout shut. The opening and shutting of the snout happens so fast that you probably wouldn't see it. But you might hear a tiny click as the snout shuts.

No Teeth, No Stomach, No Problem!

Seahorses have no teeth. They swallow whatever they eat whole. They also do not have a stomach. The food they eat passes through them very quickly. This is one reason they have to eat so much.

What Is Seahorse Family Life Like?

Seahorse family life is not like that of any other member of the animal kingdom. With other animals, it is the female who gets pregnant and lays eggs or has babies. With seahorses, the male gets pregnant and gives birth.

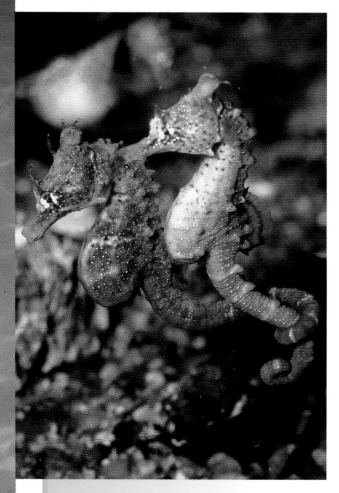

Seahorses go on "dates"

A male and female seahorse spend a lot of time together before they mate. When they meet, one or both of them may change color. Next, they may grab on to the same piece of seagrass or coral and spin around it for a time. Then they might leave the **holdfast,** link their tails together, and swim back and forth for a while. Such a "date" might last up to nine hours.

Scientists think that most **species** *of seahorse, like these shortsnouted seahorses, stay with the same partners for life.*

male's brood pouch

The female will look thinner after she puts her eggs into the male's brood pouch. The male will look fatter because his brood pouch will be full of eggs.

Males get pregnant

When two seahorses are ready to mate, the female puts her eggs in the male's brood pouch on the front of his body. The **brood pouch** is where the male **fertilizes** and then carries the eggs.

In many **species,** the female visits the male every morning while he is pregnant. The partners change color when they see each other and twirl together around a holdfast.

Fighting for a Partner

Sometimes more than two male sea pony seahorses can be interested in one female. When this happens, the males may fight. They might grab each other by the tail and wrestle. Or they might bonk each other with their **snouts.**

Babies are born

Inside the brood pouch, the fertilized eggs develop into baby seahorses in two to six weeks, depending on the **species** of seahorse. During this time, the male slowly lets seawater into the **brood pouch.** This helps the growing babies get used to the seawater before they have to swim in it.

The male usually has the babies very early in the morning. When giving birth, he squirts the babies out of his brood pouch. This can take many hours. When he is done, the male is very tired.

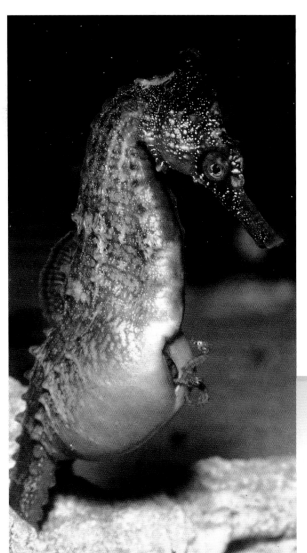

Depending on the species, a male seahorse gives birth to between 5 and more than 1,000 babies. Smaller species have fewer babies than larger species. The babies look like tiny adult seahorses. All baby seahorses are the same size. They are about one-fourth of an inch (6 millimeters) long, or about as long as a piece of rice.

A group of baby seahorses is called a brood.

Babies grow up

Baby seahorses start eating soon after they are born. The opening in a baby seahorse's **snout** is only about the size of the dot over this letter "i." So they usually eat **zooplankton** that is not full-grown.

The father and mother do not provide any care or help to baby seahorses. In fact, very soon after the birth, the parents leave to start another family. Many baby seahorses never grow up. Many end up as a meal for larger fish, crabs, or seabirds.

Baby seahorses may find a holdfast soon after they are born, or they may spend some time floating freely in the water.

It takes small seahorses, such as the dwarf seahorse, about three months to grow up. Larger species, such as the White's seahorse, take six to twelve months. Scientists aren't sure exactly how long seahorses can live. But they think that smaller species can live a year and a half. Larger species may live four to five years.

How Do Seahorses Protect Themselves

Unlike baby seahorses, adult seahorses don't have many animal **predators,** or enemies. Seahorses have some tricks that they use to make themselves almost impossible to find.

They Have Bones and Spines

Under their skin, seahorses have hard sheets of bone that protect their insides. The raised rings you see around a seahorse's body show where these sheets of bone join together. Sea creatures that try to eat seahorses usually end up spitting them out—too crunchy! After that, these creatures usually stay away from seahorses.

Some **species** of seahorse have sharp spines on their backs. Two examples are the thorny seahorse and the hedgehog seahorse. Most predators usually don't bother these prickly seahorses.

The spines on this thorny seahorse are very long and sharp. They run from the top of the seahorse's head almost to the tip of the tail.

Some species, like this pygmy seahorse, change color to match the coral they rest on.

They can blend into the background

A few predators such as crabs, skates, and even sea turtles, don't mind a little extra crunch. To keep from getting eaten by these predators, seahorses can change color to **camouflage** themselves. For example, a seahorse living in a **coral reef** can turn purple or pink to match the corals.

? Did you know?

It only takes a seahorse a few minutes to change its color to match nearby plants or coral.

Pipefishes and Seadragons

Pipefishes and sea dragons are related to seahorses. They, too, are very good at blending in. Pipefishes look like straightened out seahorses. Their ribbon-like bodies look a lot like the flat pieces of seagrass they live in. Sea dragons look like seahorses that have grown leaves. The leafy bits make sea dragons hard to tell apart from a piece of floating seaweed.

Are Seahorses Endangered?

Seahorses' worst enemies are humans, not other sea creatures. Human activities harm and destroy seahorse **habitat.** This is one reason some **species** of seahorse may become **endangered.** An endangered species is one that is in danger of dying out. Also, fishermen catch about 20 million seahorses a year. The seahorses they catch are used in medicines, made into **souvenirs,** or kept as pets. As a result, the number of seahorses in the world's oceans has fallen.

Seahorses can lose their homes

Putting up new buildings and cutting down trees along the coast can cause water pollution. This harms and destroys the **seagrass beds, coral reefs,** and **mangrove forests** where seahorses live.

In 2001, the cape seahorse became the first endangered species of seahorse. Building projects along the coast of South Africa have harmed its habitat.

These dead seahorses may be mixed with other ingredients to make medicine or used whole.

Seahorses are used in medicines

Some doctors in Asia use dead seahorses in medicines. Seahorse medicines are thought to help people with broken bones, breathing problems, heart disease, and other health problems. Seahorses cannot have babies fast enough to replace the millions caught each year for these medicines.

Seahorses are made into souvenirs

For many years, gift shops in beach areas have sold keyrings, paperweights, and jewelry made of dead seahorses. Each year hundreds of thousands of seahorses are caught and made into these souvenirs.

Seahorses are sold as pets

Seahorses seem like they would make fun pets. But keeping a seahorse alive in a home **aquarium** is very hard. Feeding them the right kind of food is one problem. They also get sick easily. Several hundred thousand seahorses are caught each year and sold as pets. Most of them die.

What Can We Do to Save Seahorses?

A group called Project Seahorse, based in Canada, is helping to save seahorses. Project Seahorse and other groups and individuals are working to help protect seahorse **habitat.** They also help people understand the dangers seahorses face and find ways to cut down on the number of seahorses caught each year.

Protect seahorse habitat

It is important to protect **seagrass beds, coral reefs,** and **mangrove forests.** This will make sure that seahorses have a place to live. Protecting these areas may mean passing laws about what kind of building is allowed in coastal areas. Laws may also be passed to control logging and other activities that cause water pollution.

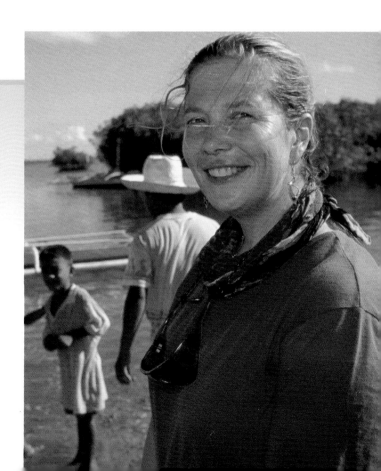

Scientist Amanda Vincent started Project Seahorse in 1996 with Heather Hall.

Some people in the Philippines now have jobs protecting seahorses.

Set aside safe places for seahorses

Setting aside an area along the coast as a safe area for seahorses can help. In these safe areas, or **sanctuaries,** catching seahorses is not allowed. This gives seahorses a secure place to have babies, and the babies can remain safe while they grow up.

At a sanctuary near the village of Handumon in the Philippines, people guard the water to make sure no one catches the seahorses that live there. Since this program began, the number of seahorses in the area has been slowly increasing.

Doctors can help, too

Project Seahorse is working with doctors in Asia who use seahorse medicines. Sometimes other ingredients can be used instead of seahorses. Or doctors can try to use seahorse **species** that are less **endangered.**

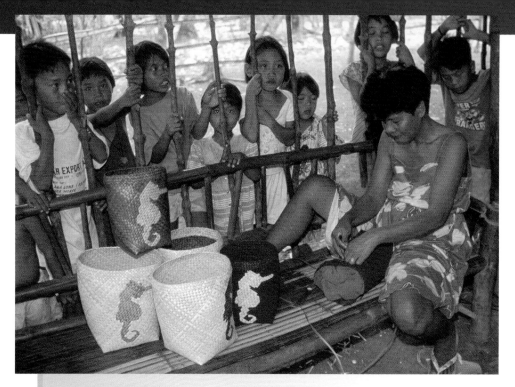

These craft items are just some of the things made and sold by people who used to catch seahorses.

Stop buying seahorses

Many people who buy **souvenirs** like seahorse keyrings don't know that seahorses are in danger. Once people know this, most will probably not buy these souvenirs. Most people also don't know that pet seahorses usually die. If they did, they would stop buying them. This could save up to half a million seahorses each year. That is why educating people about seahorses is important.

Find new jobs for seahorse fishermen

What will happen to people who make their living fishing for seahorses? Project Seahorse is helping these people find other ways to make money. In the Philippines, some fishermen now make and sell crafts with seahorse designs.

How Do We Learn about Seahorses?

Some scientists learn about seahorses by studying them in tanks. Others study seahorses in their natural **habitat.**

Scientists study captive seahorses

Seahorses kept in tanks need extra special care. The water cannot be too warm or too cool. The potbelly seahorse, for example, does best in very clean water that is 64 °F to 75°F (18 °C to 24 °C). The scientists also need to keep tanks full of live **zooplankton** to feed to the seahorses twice a day.

At the National Aquarium in Baltimore, scientist Jorge Gomezjurado **breeds** seahorses. Gomezjurado watches the pregnant males closely and writes down what he sees. He collects **data,** or information, about how many babies each male has.

Gomezjurado is breeding seahorses to give to **aquariums** around the world. This way aquariums won't have to catch wild seahorses for their displays.

Scientist Jorge Gomezjurado at the National Aquarium in Baltimore with a leafy sea dragon.

25

Scientists study wild seahorses

The first step in studying seahorses in their natural **habitat** is finding them. Once scientists find some seahorses, they may mark off the area with brightly colored tape. This will make it easier to find the seahorses the next time. Then they collect **data** about the seahorses' size, weight, and other things.

Scientists that study seahorses in the wild have to be patient. They might spend hours underwater watching one or two seahorses. They watch the seahorses to find out about many things. For example, scientists are interested in learning more about how seahorses mate. So they watch how seahorse partners act when they are together. Scientists are also interested in getting more details about how **species** of seahorse are different from each other.

Scientists put a little necklace with a number on it around a seahorse's neck. The number helps the scientists tell the seahorses apart.

The natural beauty of seahorses is reason enough to work to save them.

We still need to learn more

There are still many things we do not know about seahorses, such as how they live and act in their natural habitat. Scientists need to collect more data to better understand how the number of seahorses in the ocean has changed over the years. Scientists share what they learn with conservation groups and governments. Together they can work on the best ways to keep seahorses safe.

Seahorses are just one of the many creatures living in the ocean. They are a tiny piece of the puzzle that makes up all life on Earth. All creatures on the planet depend on each other in one way or another. The loss of any species can affect others that depend on it. Working to make sure that seahorses don't die out is one way to help keep the puzzle from falling apart.

☑ The largest seahorse is the Pacific seahorse, which can grow to be twelve inches (30 centimeters) long.

☑ Seahorses, pipefishes, and seadragons are the only animal species in which males become pregnant and give birth.

☑ Seahorses can make a clicking sound by rubbing two parts of their skull together. The sound they make sounds like fingers snapping. Scientists are not sure why seahorses make these sounds.

☑ A yellow seahorse at the National Aquarium in Baltimore gave birth to a record number of 2,020 babies.

The smallest seahorses are the dwarf seahorse and the Pygmy seahorse. Both are less than an inch (2.5 centimeters) long.

✓ A sea creature known as a pipehorse looks a little bit like a seahorse and a little bit like a pipefish. Pipehorses have tails that curl and can grab on to a **holdfast** like a seahorse. But their bodies and heads are straighter, like those of a pipefish.

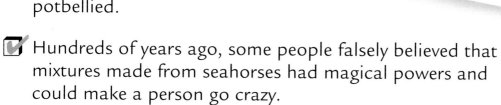

Pipefish are related to seahorses. This alligator pipefish looks almost like the seagrass it lives in.

✓ Potbelly seahorses can puff themselves up with air, making themselves look even more potbellied.

✓ Hundreds of years ago, some people falsely believed that mixtures made from seahorses had magical powers and could make a person go crazy.

✓ The cape seahorse can live in water that is two times as salty as normal ocean water. It can also live in water that has almost no salt in it.

Glossary

aquarium building where people can see sea creatures that are on display. Fish tanks are also sometimes called aquariums.

backbone bone that stretches down the middle of the back and protects the spine

breed a male and female come together to make babies

brood pouch pocket-like flap on the front part of a male seahorse's body

camouflage to change the way something looks so it won't be as easy to see

cold-blooded having blood that is the same temperature as the air or water an animal lives in

coral reef underwater formations made of the hard skeletons of millions of tiny sea animals

coronet bony growth that looks like a crown on top of a seahorse's head

crustacean type of animal that includes shrimp, lobsters, and crayfish

data facts and information

dorsal fin fin on the back part of a seahorse's body. Seahorses flap their dorsal fin to swim forward.

endangered in danger of dying out completely so that there will be no more left on Earth

fertilize make eggs able to grow and develop into babies

fin wing-shaped or fan-shaped part of a fish's body that the fish can move to help it swim

gill structure in a fish's body that the fish uses to breathe

habitat place where an animal lives in the wild

holdfast object such as a piece of seagrass or coral that a seahorse wraps its tail around

mangrove forest shallow area of water near a coast in which groups of mangrove trees grow. Mangrove tree roots arch above the surface of the water.

pectoral fin one of two fins on each side of a seahorse's neck. Seahorses use their pectoral fins to help them steer and keep their balance.

predator animal that hunts and eats another type of animal

sanctuary safe or protected place

seagrass bed grassy plants that make up a thick underwater "forest"

snout a seahorse's hollow, tube-shaped mouth

souvenir gift item that reminds people of a place they have visited

species group of animals that have the same features and can have babies with each other

zooplankton any of a number of very tiny sea animals that float in the ocean and are eaten by sea creatures, including seahorses

More Books to Read

Landau, Elaine. *Sea Horses*. Danbury, Conn.: Children's Press, 1999.

Stefoff, Rebecca. *Sea Horse*. Tarrytown, N.Y. : Benchmark Books, 1997.

Walker, Sally A. *Sea Horses*. Minneapolis, Minn.: Carolrhoda Books, 1999.

Index